The Almost Animals

by Hugh Holman

D1465333

KAJ

Published by
Strident Publishing Ltd
22 Strathwhillan Drive
The Orchard
Hairmyres
East Kilbride
G75 8GT

Tel: +44 (0)1355 220588
info@stridentpublishing.co.uk
www.stridentpublishing.co.uk

Published by Strident Publishing, 2015
Text and illustrations © Hugh Holman, 2015
Cover design by Michael Holman and Hugh Holman

A catalogue record for this book is available from the British Library.

ISBN 978-1-910829-01-1

Typeset in Century Schoolbook by Andrew Forteath
Printed by Bell & Bain

The publisher acknowledges support from Creative Scotland towards the publication of this title.

For My Family and Other Aminals

Chapter 1

Welcome to Nowhere

WELCOME TO NOWHERE

POPULATION: 146 AMINALS 187 SPECIES

IF YOU DON'T HAVE WINGS BEWARE THE DROP

Up on the land and down in the sea, the animals get on with their lives. Elephants trumpet and trample, dolphins dodge and dive, tigers purr and pose, turtles heave and ho. And each creature has its place, whether it's a forest or grassland, a desert, a sandy beach, or maybe a coral reef.

Or most do.

At the end of the land, overlooking the ocean, stands The Cliff, a mighty one hundred giraffes high. Above The Cliff, the land animals roam. Below it, the sea animals swim. But halfway up is a very unusual village. The land animals call it *The Village at the End of the World*, and the sea animals call it *The Village in the Sky*, but everyone knows it as the village of Nowhere.

And Nowhere is where the a*min*als live.

The a*min*als *are* animals, they are just a bit mixed up. They come from all over – jungles, mountains, meadows, caves – but no matter where they were born, they have all ended up in Nowhere. There is no other place for them.

Nowhere sits on narrow ledges of rock that look like giant shelves. They cling to the edge of the land.

A wooden sign on the highest ledge displays a bizarre message to passing travellers, though those are few and far between.

It reads:

> **WELCOME TO NOWHERE**
> Population: 146 a*min*als, 187 species

It goes on to say:

> IF YOU DON'T HAVE WINGS,
> BEWARE THE DROP

Most days, you will find three puffickens perching on the sign. They are best avoided unless you wish to be called rude names like Bogbrain or Wiffybottom, or even just Big Ears. You don't even need particularly large ears for them to call you that.

Their clumsy chicken heritage can make life on The Cliff quite hard for them. When they jump into the air to fly they...fall most of the way down The Cliff before their wings lift their fat bodies. Their puffin side makes it feel like home though, as they love being close to the ocean, which means being close to their favourite food: tasty sand eels.

At the centre of the village you will nearly always find the huge elephanoceros, and the equally huge rhinuffalo. You will nearly always find them *there* because they are too big to fit anywhere else. They can only *just* pass each other on the widest ledges and are unable to visit much of the village. The Cliff is perhaps not ideal for them, but with slow and careful movements, they too have made it their home.

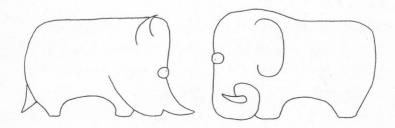

Perhaps the freest members of Nowhere are those with wings, for they can easily flap, flutter and fly anywhere they want. They can also get to the furthest ledges, which the other aminals can't reach.

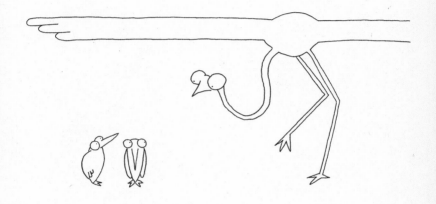

The aminals of Nowhere try to fit in as best they can. For some, such as the squats, it's been easy. Their squirrel side means they are good at climbing, and their bat heritage means they can fly. So The Cliff really isn't a problem for them at all.

But for others, life in Nowhere has been rather more challenging.

Chapter 2

The Always Pond

On the very lowest ledge of the village, there
is a large pool, roughly the shape of a shoe.
Two eyes slowly emerge from the surface,
look around, then, with an underwater sigh
that causes bubbles to rise to the surface,
sink back down again.

There are few places to be fully on your own in Nowhere, but one such place is The Always Pond. Other puddles come and go with the weather, but, as its name suggests, The Always Pond is always there. It is filled by a natural spring that seeps through The Cliff.

Only one member of the village can stay underwater long enough to enjoy the peace and quiet The Always Pond can bring: Angle the young crocogator.

Angle is the unhappiest a*min*al in Nowhere.

If she lets herself sink until her scaly belly is resting on the bottom of The Always Pond, Angle's world is calm and shadowy. That might sound wonderful to some, but Angle wants chaos and clarity. She doesn't want peace and quiet, she wants to play and be loud and have fun with all the others.

The one time that she tried to play with a lemurdillo, it curled up into a ball so fast that it nearly rolled off the side of The Cliff. Another time, she tried to join in a game with a group of frogmeleons, but they just kept changing colour until she left. (Angle doesn't know this, but they also stuck their tongues out at her after she'd gone.)

She doesn't mind the other youngsters being afraid of her teeth, and she doesn't even mind very much when they call her names, like Snaggletooth the Swamp Monster, because at least, then, she feels included in a small way. What she does mind, though, is being ignored. She doesn't like being treated like an outsider in what has become her home.

The problem is this: the aminals arrive in Nowhere because they don't fit in with other animals. They are pushed out of their homes. Forced to find somewhere else to live, they eventually make their way to Nowhere.

Angle's troubles are a little different from those of the other *amin*als. A crocodile looks rather like an alligator, and an alligator looks rather like a crocodile. So while Angle is an *amin*al as much as any other in Nowhere, she certainly doesn't look like one.

As if to rub it in, when Angle surfaces once more, a family of hoggits hop past, looking absurd with their huge ears and feet, with spiky backs and long snuffling noses. None of them even looks in Angle's direction. Why can't *she* look that unusual? Or perhaps the problem is that, here, she *is* the one that looks unusual.

She ponders this thought with a melancholy swish of her tail, and dreams of Elsewhere.

Chapter 3

A sudden and shocking decision

As the sun nudges its way above the horizon, the ocean becomes orange. Light once more spills into the world.

The aminals always have a marvellous view of the sunrise. It is one of the best things about living in Nowhere. Unless you're a cattoon. Cattoons hate the sunrise because it means it's bedtime.

From The Always Pond, Angle watches the ocean—The Forever Pond, as it is known in Nowhere—expand towards her. Some way in the distance, a pod of dolphins appears. They jump and play and move with such grace and ease that she can't help but be jealous. Could *she* swim that fast if she had enough space? Her tail twitches with excitement as she imagines swimming in that giant pool far below.

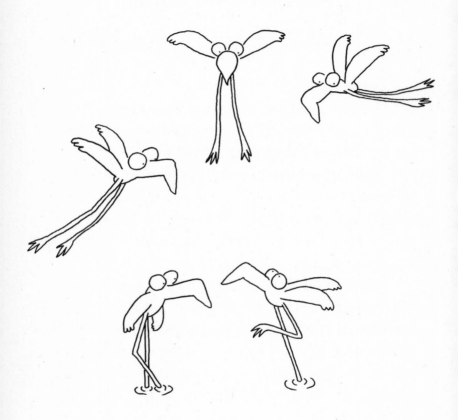

For a few minutes, a group of tiny, pink flummingbirds hovers over The Always Pond, scooping up water with their upturned beaks. Their wings leave a tiny humming noise in the air. One whispers, 'Watch out for that crocodile!'

The flummingbirds flutter away as Nowhere's only snortoise arrives at the water's edge, as he does at this time every day, to take his morning drink. He gives Angle an elongated look, before slowly turning and slide-plodding away. Angle is sure that the snortoise would prefer it if she weren't there.

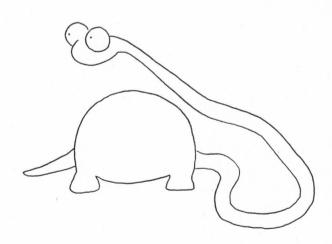

A tiny speck of movement in the distant sky catches her eye. It is Tupi the toulican. The dot grows into the familiar flapping shape, and Angle notices that his little wings look as if they struggle to carry his massive bill through the air. Being half pelican means he is extremely good at fishing, and today he is carrying a hefty load. If Angle had lips, she would be licking them right now. But she hasn't, so she doesn't.

Tupi fetches food for all the aminals that eat fish. She wishes he would come to her ledge first, but every time he starts at the top and works his way down. He never ever forgets to save her some fish, even if she doesn't have the best choice of the catch.

After a little while, Tupi drops onto the lowest ledge. With a rather disgusting splat, he empties the rest of the fish from his bill. 'There you go, Angle,' he says in a warm but weary voice.

Angle is already climbing out of the water. 'Thank you,' she replies. 'I'm so hungry!'

Tupi is able to smile now that his bill isn't full of fish, and he does so as he turns to leave.

'Wait!' Angle calls. 'You fly a long way from Nowhere, don't you?'

Turning back, Tupi says that he does, and adds, 'I go as far as I need so that no aminal goes hungry.'

'And you see other animals?' she asks, eagerly.

'I do,' he murmurs cautiously, ruffling his wing feathers.

'What are they like?'

The toulican sighs and waddles towards the edge. His webbed feet make a wet slapping noise with each step. *Slap, slap, slap.* He looks out into the distance. 'Some animals are friendly. Others...are less so. Most are confused by me. They don't understand a*min*als.'

Angle creeps further forwards, so just her tail and back legs are still in the water. 'But we're animals just like them, aren't we?' she asks hopefully.

'Hmmm,' Tupi begins. 'Angle, in some ways we are all completely the same; but in other ways, we are not.'

He doesn't appear to have anything else to say, and Angle can see that he's tired and wants to leave. Probably to go back to his hollow, high up on The Cliff, to have a nap.

He readies himself at the edge of the ledge and only halts when a small voice asks—

'Would I have a place there, a long way from Nowhere?'

Tupi's head swivels and, for the first time in the conversation, he really *looks* at her. 'Angle, Nowhere is the place for a*min*als.' With that, he launches himself and clumsily flaps away.

Even though Angle was very hungry a few moments ago, the fish lie uneaten in front of her.

The Forever Pond is still and silent, and there are no a*min*als or animals in sight. Nowhere might be the place for a*min*als, but it doesn't seem to be the place for *her*. Faint noise drifts down from the rest of the village; her only reminder that she's not completely on her own. She hears one voice shout, louder than the rest:

'Not down there, that's where that alligator lives!'

As she gazes out to the ocean, Angle decides she is going to make a sudden and shocking decision.

But she knows that important decisions shouldn't be made with an empty stomach, so she gobbles up all the tasty fish, and doesn't lick her lips afterwards. Because she still doesn't have any.

Then, Angle makes her sudden and shocking decision.

She will leave Nowhere, to go Somewhere.

Chapter 4

Up!

Up, up, up!

Up is the only option, thinks Angle, as she considers her travels. The Forever Pond was her first thought, but there is no way down The Cliff. To anyone brave enough to peer over the edge, the beach is sometimes visible as a thin, pale strip far below. But a lot of the time it is hidden by a thick blanket of fog, which rolls in with the tide.

It is a legendary place amongst non-flying aminals, as only those with wings can visit the beach. Sometimes they tell stories about seeing amazing things, like the day hundreds of squidgy jellyfish appeared, or the time the water glowed like the moon.

Angle would love to visit the beach and see these strange things for herself and, of course, swim with the dolphins. She gazes over the side of her ledge and strains her eyes, trying to see any kind of movement below. There is no fog today, but, as usual, she still can't see anything.

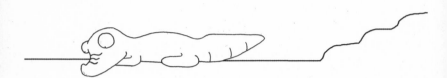

A pair of wingless villagers named Marlowe and Wimmy claim that there are mermaids down in The Forever Pond. Marlowe and Wimmy are odgers – half otter and half badger. Everyone calls them the Old Codgers. It doesn't bother them though. Nothing does really.

They live a little way above Angle, in a small tunnel behind a ledge. It is this ledge where The Sometimes Pond can sometimes be found. When it's filled, they swim in it; when it's not, they don't. Sometimes, if there is a long dry spell, they will stroll down to

The Always Pond. Angle enjoys these visits, but they don't happen very often.

Although she doesn't believe in mermaids, these stories make Angle very curious about the world beyond Nowhere.

The Old Codgers have told Angle everything she knows about crocodiles and alligators. Unlike everyone else, they never mistake her for one or the other. Some youngsters mostly call her an alligator, but nearly all the grown-ups call her a crocodile, even Tupi the toulican. So when he told her "Nowhere is the place for a*min*als," he was accidentally convincing her that she should leave.

Angle will miss his familiar face with its saggy fish-carrying bill, but even he isn't really her friend. She will miss the Old Codgers the most, and hopes to see them on her way up, to say goodbye and perhaps ask for some tips for her adventure.

Tomorrow, she decides. Tomorrow will be the day that she goes up, up, up, and leaves Nowhere in search of a new home. Perhaps as a crocodile, since that's what she is most often mistaken for—by *amin*als that should probably know better.

Angle will have to climb through the village. Climbing is hard work, as she has short legs and isn't very good at jumping.

Some of the ledges of rock are connected by wooden walkways. Who, or what, constructed them, and why, has long since been forgotten, but they have become important for villagers like Angle who aren't good climbers. There are also some ropes and ladders, but Angle knows she won't be able to use them.

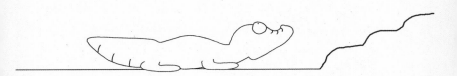

For the rest of the day – her last in the village – Angle stays either at the surface of the water or on the ledge. Today, she doesn't want to hide herself away. Today, she is daydreaming about the land above The Cliff. Will she find a new family? Will she make some friends? Perhaps they will take her to The Forever Pond, and then maybe, just maybe, she can swim with the dolphins.

Happy in these thoughts, she slips back into her pool as the light starts to fade, barely causing a ripple to break the surface of the dark water.

Chapter 5

Climbing The Cliff

It is still dark when Angle wakes, though a slight glow on the horizon tells her that dawn is not far away. The air isn't cold, but the water has slowly drained her energy through the night. She sluggishly crawls out of The Always Pond and allows the gentle morning heat to wake her.

As she warms up, she starts to worry about her plans to leave. Is it the right decision? Maybe she should just stay here after all. It hasn't been *that* bad living in Nowhere.

Out of the corner of her eye, she notices that the snortoise is at the edge of the pond. Water drips from his mouth as he gulps. They stare at each other for a few moments before he turns and disappears without a word.

Angle's mind is made up. She is leaving.

As the day breaks, The Forever Pond turns orange, then green and then blue. That's what mornings normally do. In Nowhere, anyway.

But for once, Angle is not gazing out at the giant pool below. Instead, she is lying on the ledge, looking at The Always Pond. *Her* pond. It is so familiar to her, but today it seems so different. She is too excited to feel sad for long. Her tail twitches anxiously from side to side.

Angle gently touches the water with her foot, and watches the ripples spread across The Always Pond. She bows her head, for just a moment, before turning and heading up, up, up.

There are a few small steps to get to the next ledge. She can just about heave herself up with her little legs. Her scales and tough skin protect her body as it scrapes against the stone.

The next ledge is much larger than hers and sticks out further, cutting her off from the rest of the village.

She pauses briefly at the edge.

A trio of deerkats freeze and stare at her. One of them is clearly being awkwardly poked by another's antlers, but still, they all remain motionless.

A hegpie leaps into the air with a sigh and flaps away.

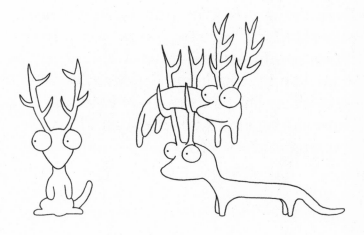

Angle makes her way across to the steps on the other side. The deerkats don't move at all. Not one muscle. But as soon as she starts climbing again she can hear muffled whispers behind her, and a loud 'Ouch! Be careful with those things!'

The next ledge seems smaller at first, but it's actually just the front of a large cave, hollowed out of The Cliff. There are many more aminals in here, and Angle isn't used to all the noise and the smells. There are growls and squeaks and whoops and purrs. There are also whiffs and stinks and tangs and pongs, but Angle doesn't want to think about those.

Unseen, for the moment, Angle watches a group of goanies standing in the centre. Even though they are quite small, aren't all white, and have two large curled horns, everyone always calls them the unicorns. (The goanies like being called unicorns because it sounds more glamorous than being part goat and part pony). They are chatting with two figers.

Angle has seen the figers once before, and thinks that they are beautiful. They are the same shape as their fox ancestors, but their colours and pattern are just like a tiger's. Well, so the Old Codgers say anyway. Angle has never seen a tiger.

She notices the family of spiky hoggits hopping around underneath the legs of the larger aminals, and hopes that no one has ever accidentally sat on one. Although the cave seems rather chaotic, everyone seems to know how it works and what to do. *It's almost like a village within a village,* Angle thinks.

Over in the corner, a large orangupanda

sits in silence, clutching a bunch of bamboo like a walking stick. For a few minutes, he is the only villager looking at Angle. His eyes seem too close together on his wide face, but they are intelligent. And he looks like he would give good hugs.

Many young *amin*als are running round
and round the floor of the cave, and their
laughter is echoing off the walls. Angle
wishes she could play with them. Although
there was that time when she accidentally
nearly swallowed a shrewsel that panicked
and tried to hide in her mouth.

Above everyone, the squats scurry and
fly around the ceiling of the cave, making
little squeaking noises.

The youngsters are the first to react
when they see Angle. They stop and stare
at her. Some of them whisper. Some of them
disappear to find their parents. It's when
the parents and the other *amin*als realise
that the youngsters have stopped running
around that they also notice her. In one
sweeping wave of stillness, the life and
energy of the village-within-a-village is lost,
and Angle becomes the centre of attention.

Angle would rather someone said
something – *anything* – than get these blank
stares from all these different eyes. Big eyes,
small eyes, wide-apart eyes, close-together
eyes, green eyes, white eyes, bright eyes.

Angle's tail starts to twitch. She keeps her head down and ambles as fast as she can across the cave to the Old Codgers' tunnel. Gratefully, she slips inside.

'Hello!' she calls. 'Marlowe? Wimmy?' There is no answer, and a brief inspection of the tunnel and The Sometimes Pond reveals that the Old Codgers are not at home.

'I'm ever so sorry,' says a tiny voice, that she almost doesn't hear, 'but Mr and Mrs Odger are not here. Can I take a message for you?'

Angle looks around to see where the voice is coming from.

'Please leave your message after the squeak.'

'But where are—'

'Squeak!'

'I can't see you!' Angle says, straining her eyes in the dim light.

'I'm over here. Now, about this message...'

Angle spies a tiny spot of blue on the wall of the tunnel. When she looks closely, she can see what appears to be a snail. A blue snail. A bright blue, stripy snail.

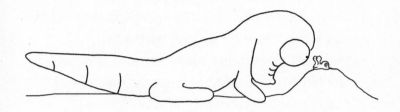

'Oh, hello,' Angle says, glad to finally put a face to the voice.

'Pleased to meet you,' squeaks the snail. 'What is your message?'

'No, I don't have a message, I just want to see the Odgers.'

'Oh I'm afraid you can't do that.'

'Where are they?' Angle has to concentrate hard to hear the tiny voice.

'They are on holiday. Would you like to leave a message?'

'No, thank you,' says Angle, and adds, 'Please stop asking me that.'

'Will that be all then?' asks the small creature.

'No…well, yes I suppose so,' says Angle. 'But where have they gone?'

The little voice replies, 'I'm afraid it is not my place to share that information. But if you would like to leave a message…'

Angle is sure that she can see a hopeful expression on the snail's face. 'That's okay', she finally says, sighing as she does so. 'Sorry for snapping at you. I'm Angle, I live down in The Always Pond.'

'Oh quite all right, Alice, quite all right. If you're friends with the Odgers, you're friends with me. I'm Spriglet.'

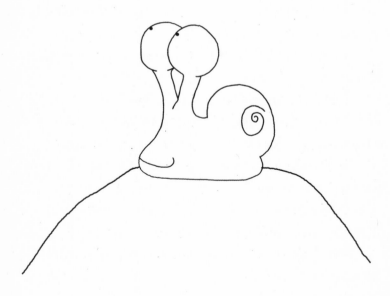

Angle can definitely see a smile now. 'I've never seen such a beautiful snail before,' she says, before quickly continuing, 'I mean, I've never seen such a blue snail before. Oh, and my name is Angle, not Alice.'

'Oh I'm not a snail,' says the non-snail. 'I'm half sea slug!'

'And what's your other half?' asks Angle.

'Well, a snail of course!'

'I see, and what kind of a*minal* does that make you?'

'I'm Spriglet!'

Angle decides to leave the conversation at that. 'Well it was lovely to meet you. You're my favourite blue snail. Now I'm going to leave Nowhere forever.'

'Okay, bye bye then, Alice!' says Spriglet cheerily.

I must get to the top of The Cliff, thinks Angle, as she leaves the Old Codgers' tunnel after her strange exchange with Spriglet.

The cave becomes silent once again, and Angle is sure that they have all been waiting for her to come back out. Without looking up, she walks across to a large wooden plank over which she can escape. She makes her mind up that she will not stop again until she reaches the top. Unless she needs to catch her breath of course. Some of it is very steep. And, her legs are ever so short.

Angle slowly climbs through the village. She reaches one ledge which has a small, thorny shrub growing through a crack in the rock. It has beautiful pink flowers on it, and they smell wonderful. No plants grow on the bottom ledges, so Angle isn't used to seeing them.

A little further up, another ledge has another pink-flowered shrub. Angle sticks her snout in and sniffs deeply.

'Oi! Crocodile! What do you think you're doing!'

The flummingbirds scatter into the air and flutter away, leaving a green, flowerless shrub.

Later, Angle turns a corner and surprises two pavarrultures that squawk and fly out of her way.

But she is able to avoid most of the other aminals by using the smaller pathways. She even manages to miss out the central hub of the village, where the elephanoceros and the rhinuffalo live their slow and careful lives.

There's only one ledge that she can climb onto the land from, though, and that means going past the puffickens...

Chapter 6

The Crocodile River

'*Where* are you going, Pondweed?' asks the first pufficken.

'Where are *you* going, Chompy Chops?' asks the second.

'Where are you *going*, you half-baked green bean?' asks the third.

WELCOME TO NOWHERE
POPULATION: 146 AMINALS 187 SPECIES

IF YOU DON'T HAVE WINGS BEWARE THE DROP

'I'm going to find my home!' replies Angle, without the slightest twitch of her tail.

'Doesn't she know where her home is?' asks the second pufficken.

'Next she'll be saying she doesn't know where her tail is!' laughs the third.

'I know where my tail is!' snaps Angle. 'It's behind me!'

'And that's exactly where your home is, little Angle,' replies the first pufficken, before all three of them burst into what seems to be an improvised song about living in Nowhere.

'Oh we don't live on the land, and we don't live in the sea,
We live here on The Cliff, with him and you and me—'

While they're distracted with their boisterous singing, Angle quietly crawls past them. With one last heave, she hauls herself onto the land and leaves The Cliff behind.

Her first thought is that The Forever Pond looks even larger from up this high, and she now fully understands its name.

One day she *will* swim in it.

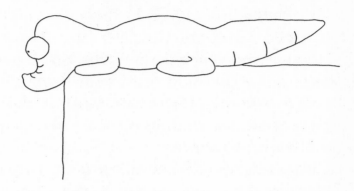

For now though, she is going to find the crocodiles!

She begins walking along the top of The Cliff. Once the puffickens' singing fades, she truly feels like she has left Nowhere behind and entered Elsewhere.

'Now, where do the crocodiles live?' she asks herself. Marlowe once told her. She can hear his warm voice in her head as she remembers what he said: "In the river to the west. There's a waterfall further along the coast, and they live upstream of that."

'Right then,' says Angle. 'Off I go.'

She is happy at first. The sun is shining, and the lovely, soft grass under her feet is much, much nicer than the hard, rocky ledge she's used to.

She walks and walks and walks. She's never walked this much before.

'Hello, I'm Angle the crocodile,' she says out loud, while she's on her own. She likes the sound of that and thinks she'll enjoy being a crocodile. If she can ever find the other crocodiles, that is. It seems like she's been walking forever!

Actually, maybe the sun is a bit *too* hot. And maybe the soft grass is making her legs *just a bit* tired. If she were back on her ledge, she could slip into The Always Pond and cool down.

For a moment, Angle stops and closes her eyes. She imagines herself back in her pool, and can almost feel the refreshing water on her back, and the taste of it in her mouth. She can even hear it splashing around. Wait, she actually *can* hear it!

Which means that the waterfall must be just up ahead. But, even closer than that, Angle spots a small boulder. Hoping she might be able to rest briefly in its shade, she makes her way towards it. But something doesn't seem quite right. Should a boulder have fur?

'Hello?' she says. 'Are you a furry boulder?'

The boulder *slowly* twists round and a head *slowly* appears and two eyes *slowly* blink. A wide mouth opens just below the eyes.

'Are... *you*... a... furry... boulder?' asks the wide mouth.

'Well, no,' says Angle. 'I'm not even furry.'

'How... do... you... know?' asks the boulder.

Angle has never met anyone who talks the way this boulder does. It's not that the words are slow, it's that it seems to take a long time to prepare each word before saying it. 'I don't have any fur on me,' she replies.

'Well... you're... not... a... very... unusual... boulder... then... are... you?'

'I'm not a boulder, I thought *you* were a boulder,' says Angle.

The boulder blinks slowly several times. 'But... I'm... not... a... boulder. I'm... a... sloth.'

'Oh sorry,' says Angle. 'I don't know much about sloths, but aren't you supposed to live in a tree?'

The sloth turns its head *slowly* round to the right, then *slowly* round to the left. Then it faces Angle again and blinks heavily. 'This... is... a... tree.'

Angle also looks round to the left and then the right, then back at the sloth. 'No it's not, we're at the top of The Cliff!' She hopes she didn't sound rude saying that, but it really had to be said.

The sloth seems to ponder this for a long time.

'But... I... climbed... up... a... brown... bit... and... now... I'm... in... the... green... bit... at... the... top.' He then adds: 'I... like... this... tree...' and smiles broadly.

Angle smiles too. 'Well, I'm impressed you climbed up so high,' she says. 'I'm trying to reach the waterfall so I can swim up the river and find the crocodiles.'

'Ah... yes... I... saw... the... waterfall. I'm... afraid... it... is... a... very... very... long... way... away.'

'Really? I think I can hear it though,' says Angle.

'Oh... yes. It... will... take... ages... to... reach... it,' warns the sloth.

Angle looks past the sloth and can definitely see the edge of the river as it cascades off the side of The Cliff. 'It's just over there,' she says.

'Don't... let... appearances... deceive...

you. I... often... think... I... have... nearly...
arrived... but... then... I... see... that...
I've... barely... left.'

Angle can't wait to cool off in the water.
'Well, I must be going,' she says. 'It was
lovely to meet you.' With one last smile, she
scurries towards the waterfall as quickly as
her tired legs can carry her.

'I'll... come... too,' calls the sloth. 'I'll...
catch... you... up.'

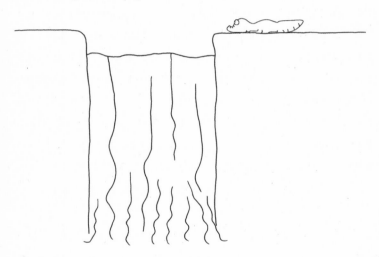

Angle wants to jump straight into the river,
but the water is white and frothy as it shoots
off the side of the land. Angle is a good
swimmer, but she doesn't fancy being swept
over the edge. She forces herself to continue

walking and follow the river inland. After all, it's better to have sore legs than to *fall* down a water*fall!*

When the river looks calmer, and she can't stop herself any longer, she slides down the river bank and into the refreshing water. Her aching legs are soothed, and her dusty scales are washed. She feels like a new crocogator. *Crocodile*, she corrects herself.

At first, she swims slowly and carefully, out of habit. But look at all the space she has! She thrusts her tail back and forth, and propels herself up the river as quickly as possible. It feels amazing! With her legs flat against her sides, she zigs and zags and zooms, faster and faster. She even tries to jump like she's seen the dolphins do in The Forever Pond, but finds it quite tricky.

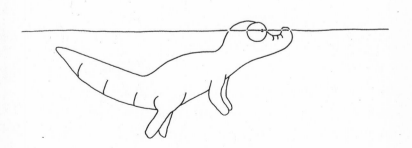

When her tail starts to feel worn out,
she lets herself sink to the river bed. It feels
different from being in The Always Pond,
where the water is always still. She closes
her eyes and enjoys the feeling of the water
moving slowly over her head.

But when she opens them again, she is
not alone. There are eight eyes, all a bit like
her own, and sixteen legs, also a bit like her
own. There are four long snouts, and...*lots* of
teeth.

Four huge crocodiles!

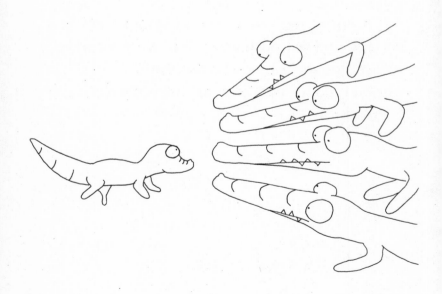

'Hello!' Her voice sounds funny underwater, slower and muffled, and she is a little bit scared. 'I'm so pleased to see you,' she says. 'I came here to find you!'

'Why?' asks one crocodile, in a deep voice that Angle can actually *feel* through the water.

Angle wasn't expecting this question. She thought it would be obvious. 'Umm...I think this might be where I belong,' she replies, suddenly feeling shy, as well as a little bit scared.

A different crocodile responds. 'You do not belong here, a*mina*l!'

A third crocodile adds, 'You are no crocodile! Look at your snout! Leave this place! Leave this place now!'

Angle turns and flees, trying to hide her tears. They are most certainly not crocodile tears.

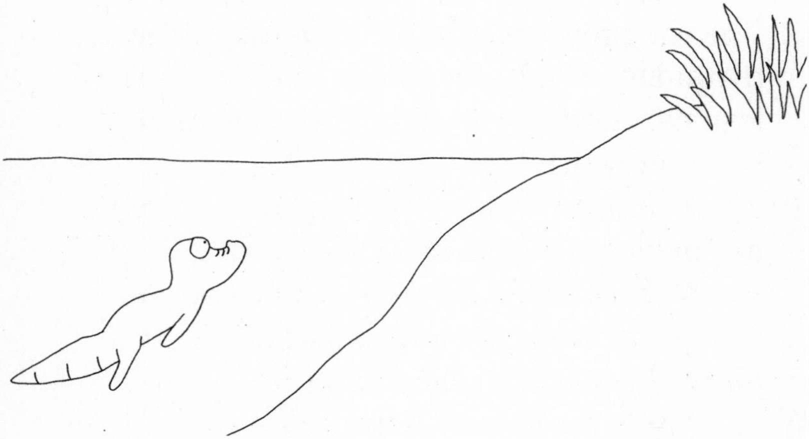

Chapter 7

Under The Hiding Bush

With her legs once again flat against her sides, Angle whips her tail back and forth and swims as fast as she can to the riverbank, where she scampers up and away from the water. Then she does a very un-crocodile thing: she hides under a bush. She expected the crocodiles to come chasing after her, but they don't seem to have bothered.

Angle doesn't understand why the crocodiles were horrible to her. They didn't even want to get to know her. *Why didn't they give me a chance?* she wonders.

Maybe it's because I am really an alligator. That must be it! If I'm not a crocodile I simply must *be an alligator!* 'I didn't want to be a crocodile anyway,' she mutters to herself.

Angle remembers very clearly that

the alligators live in a large swamp called
The Muddy Marsh, somewhere to the east.
She remembers the name because she
always thought it sounded like a fun place.
Although she doesn't know exactly where it
is, she knows that she travelled west to find
the crocodiles, so she should be able to work
out where she needs to go next.

A high-pitched voice suddenly speaks
from right next to her.

Angle jumps, but when she looks round
she is thrilled to see that it's an *amina*l! A
creature, clearly half beaver, half duck, is
sitting beside her.

'Hello!' says Angle. 'What are you? A

deaver maybe? A buck?'

'How rude,' the creature replies. 'You should never ask someone what they are. No, no, no, certainly not. Especially when that someone was just about to save you from those crocodiles.'

'Sorry,' says Angle. 'But I didn't really need saving from them. I *am* a crocodile... sort of.'

'Don't be so silly, of course you're not. You are silly. Anyway, my name is Puddle, and I'm a platypus.'

'A platypus?' Angle has never heard of a platypus, and the name doesn't make any sense to her. 'Why don't you live in

Nowhere?' she asks.

'Nowhere?' repeats Puddle, 'Nowhere? Why would I live in Nowhere? What a silly thing to say. Why don't *you* live in Nowhere, huh?'

'I do!' exclaims Angle. 'Well...I did,' she adds quietly, her tail slowly curling round her.

Puddle's voice becomes softer, though still very high-pitched. 'What are you doing here then?'

Angle tells Puddle that she's finding a new home where she'll fit in.

'But you're not a crocodile! How silly you are if you think you're a crocodile!' says Puddle.

Angle is not sure how to respond to this. In fact, she's not sure what to make of Puddle at all. A platypus? Whatever a platypus is, it has wide-apart eyes, stubby legs with webbed feet, and smooth brown fur. And of course, a duck mouth and a beaver tail. It also seems to use the word 'silly' rather a lot.

Angle blinks her eyes and twitches her tail on the dusty ground. 'Well where do *you* live then?' she asks, eventually.

Puddle sighs. It's her turn to blink and twitch her tail. Angle notices that Puddle's tail goes up and down, not side to side like her own.

'I'm not sure where I live,' says Puddle. 'My mama and I kept moving from place to place, but we could never seem to find anywhere we could call home. My mama's not here anymore.'

Puddle lets out two small sobs and her duck-mouth clatters open and shut a few times.

'I'm very sorry,' says Angle. 'I think I know how you feel. I'm on my own as well.'

Puddle slowly shakes her head. 'It's sad that we're both on our own.'

Angle nods. 'Yes, I wish we had someone we could talk to.'

Puddle blinks and twitches her tail up and down.

Angle blinks and twitches her tail from side to side.

'Wait a minute!' says Angle suddenly. 'You're not on your own, and I'm not on my own either. And we're talking to each other!'

Puddle claps her duck-mouth happily. *Clap, clap, clap.* 'You're right! We're not alone!'

Angle can't help but smile as she thinks of an idea. 'Maybe we could find a home together? I'm going to The Muddy Marsh. It's a swamp.'

Puddle's duck-mouth bends into a smile. 'Really? Oh I would like that very much! The Muddy Marsh you say? That sounds like a lot of fun. It's so lovely to meet you. What's your name?'

'My name is Angle…and I am *not* a crocodile.'

Chapter 8

Grassland games

Angle suggests that the best way to find The Muddy Marsh is probably to follow the river.

'Yes,' agrees Puddle. 'Mama always said that water leads to water.'

After a short walk, the river starts to curve to the west. Since Angle knows that the swamp is somewhere east, they decide to leave it behind and head across the land. The grass is very short to begin with, but the further they travel, the longer it gets.

As they walk side by side, they quickly notice that they share a very similar waddle. Angle reckons it's because they both prefer being in the water to being on the land. Puddle's feet remind Angle of Tupi the toulican. They both have webbed feet that slap the ground when they walk. *Slap, slap, slap.*

The grass is the same height as them now, and getting even taller, but they stay close so they can still see each other. Angle is enjoying having someone to talk to, and she suspects that Puddle feels the same way. They certainly have a lot to chat about! Angle talks about Nowhere, and the Old Codgers, and the mermaids, and anything she can think of.

Puddle likes the sound of the ocean. 'Mama never let me go near The Cliff, so I've never seen it. Maybe we could go there?'

Angle is tempted. It would be nice to

show off The Forever Pond, and point out some dolphins. But she really wants to find The Muddy Marsh. That's where she belongs, she's sure of it.

'I still can't believe you haven't been to Nowhere!' says Angle.

Puddle frowns. 'Why would I have been?'

'Because you're—'

At that moment, a loud snorting noise stops them in their tracks. They can't see where the sound came from through the grass.

Angle looks at Puddle.

Puddle looks at Angle. 'I'm scared,' she says, her voice even higher than normal. Her duck-mouth judders.

'Me too,' answers Angle.

Another snort! The grass begins to shake.

'Shall we run?' asks Puddle.

The snorting, squelching noise is closer now.

'Which direction?' shouts Angle.

But it's too late. The grass in front of them rattles wildly, and out of it leaps...*a giant snarling monster!*

Well, it isn't really a giant. It's only slightly larger than Angle and Puddle.

A small snarling monster!

Well, it isn't really a monster, it's really just an odd-looking animal.

A small snarling animal!

Although, it isn't really snarling now. It's saying, 'Hello, friends! Nice to meet you!'

The animal looks from Angle to Puddle and back with big eyes full of happiness. His long tongue is hanging from his open mouth, and his ears flop from side to side as he moves his head. Above his mouth is a large round snout.

Angle and Puddle burst out laughing! To think, a few seconds ago, they had been terrified!

'What's...your...name...?' spurts Puddle, between chuckles.

'Well, I'm Hamley,' he says bounding over to them. 'What are your names?'

'I'm Angle,' says Angle.

'I'm Puddle,' says Puddle.

'Angle and Puddle. What great names! Where are you off to, friends? Say, you're not on an adventure are you?' His mouth flops open into a lopsided smile.

'We're going to find a swamp,' answers Puddle.

'A swamp? Well there's one not too far away,' says Hamley.

'There is?' asks Angle, happily. 'Could you take us there?'

Hamley yelps with joy and jumps up and down. 'Of course! Anything for my new friends. And how about we play a game on the way?'

Angle remembers the other youngsters playing in Nowhere, and how they stared at her and never asked her to join in.

But now here she is, with two friends wanting to play. They're not scared of her teeth, and they're calling her by her name. Her real name. Not Swamp Monster, or Stumpy Legs, or Dinobore, but her actual name!

'Come on Angle, run!' calls Puddle, as she waddles off quickly into the grass.

First of all, Angle and Puddle have to go and hide while Hamley tries to find them. It doesn't take long. Then Hamley and Puddle hide. It takes Angle a very long time to find them. When she finally does, she and Hamley go and hide, while Puddle looks for them.

Angle finds out that Hamley is a pog. His father is a pig and his mother is a dog. This means he has an incredible sense of smell, which is why he was able to find her and Puddle so quickly.

'There you are!' squeaks Puddle from behind them. 'Your turn, Hamley. Quick, Angle, let's go and hide!'

Hamley flops his ears over his eyes and starts counting down. 'Twenty hippopotamus. Nineteen hippopotamus. Eighteen hippopotamus...'

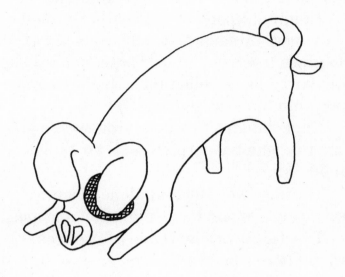

Angle and Puddle run away as fast as they can (which isn't very fast), and hide under a bush.

'This is how we first met,' whispers Puddle excitedly. Her high-pitched voice sounds funny when she tries to whisper, and they have to stop themselves laughing.

'Coming! Ready or not!' calls Hamley.

Almost immediately, he bursts out of the grass towards them. 'There you are!' he oink-barks as he rolls under the bush and flops onto his side, panting heavily.

Angle laughs. She is having such a good time that she has forgotten all about The Muddy Marsh.

'Hamley, were you all alone when we found you? Do you have a family?' she asks.

'I certainly do,' he replies. 'They're around here somewhere, I'm sure. We're never really apart, even when we're on our own. That's the best thing about being in a family.'

Angle very much likes the sound of that. 'Why don't you live in Nowhere though?'

'Oh, Nowhere! I've heard of that place! The Village at the End of the World. Is that where all those aminals are?' he asks.

'Yes,' replies Angle. 'A*min*als like you and me and Puddle.'

Puddle *humphs* loudly.

Hamley rolls onto his legs and stands up. 'Well, everyone keeps telling me to go and live there, but I just have so much fun wherever I go. I don't mind where I am really!'

Angle has never met anyone so enthusiastic about everything before.

She likes Hamley's curly tail, which never seems to stop wagging. 'I'm glad we met you, Hamley.'

'Well, that's great! And now it's your turn, little Angle. Come on, Puddle!'

The platypus and the pog disappear off into the grass, leaving Angle to count down under the bush. 'Twenty elephanoceros. Nineteen elephanoceros. Eighteen elephanoceros...'

Through her whole life, Angle has been better at hiding than at finding friends. *But today it's for a game that I'm part of!* she thinks.

She wishes she had Hamley's sense of smell. It would make finding him and Puddle much easier. *It must be great being a pog!* she imagines.

All she can do is amble through the long grass, listening out for sounds. After a long time without any clues, she considers giving up and calling out for them.

But then she hears noises up ahead. She smirks – as much as a crocogator can smirk – and crawls forward as quietly as she can until she's in position. She readies herself; then; using her tail and back legs, she springs through the grass with a loud, 'Aha!'...

...and lands at the side of a swamp that is packed full of alligators.

Chapter 9

The Alligator Swamp

The alligators are sunbathing on the shore, and swimming in the swamp, and talking in groups, and generally doing things that alligators do. There are huge ones, and small ones, and whole families.

Most animals would be scared amongst so many alligators.

Angle isn't most animals though.

'The Muddy Marsh!' she exclaims, loudly. The closest alligators turn and look at her, but then scowl and look away.

The swamp isn't nearly as muddy as Angle expected. True, the water is the brownest she's ever seen, but then she's used to the ocean, which is orange or green or blue, but never brown.

Angle thinks there is a bare strip of land around the edge of the swamp, a bit like a beach. She's not sure though, because it's covered in alligators. With the sun shining down, it actually looks rather beautiful. *This could be my home,* she thinks.

'Hello!' she calls, ambling forward and trying to get their attention.

Again, no response. Maybe she needs to be louder. Maybe alligators don't have very good hearing.

She is about to try again, when a whispering voice from behind her says, 'Angle, don't go out there, you're not an alligator.'

It's Puddle. She and Hamley are huddled

together at the edge of the grass.

'But this can be my new home!' says
Angle brightly. 'Look at those families over
there. And the swamp, look at the swamp!
It's not even that muddy! Come and say hello
with me.'

Puddle frowns. Her duck-mouth bends
downwards. 'But you're not an alligator,
Angle.'

'It's true,' says Hamley. 'You don't smell

the same as those alligators. My nose never lies. You're not one of them, Angle.' As if to prove his point, Hamley sniffs loudly, which makes a bit of a squelching noise. 'Yep,' he confirms, 'not an alligator.'

'And *we* can't go out there,' adds Puddle, quietly.

Angle notices that Puddle's voice isn't funny like the last time she tried whispering. She also notices just how frightened they both look. Shouldn't they be happy for her? They both know how important family is, so why don't they want her to be with hers?

'Well if you're too scared to come with me, then I guess this is goodbye.'

Hamley's eyes well up and his snout starts to tremble. 'But we're your friends, Angle.'

'Well *they* can be my friends. And my family,' she snaps.

Puddle's duck-mouth clicks together several times and she looks at Hamley and back to Angle. 'Why don't you just stay with us?' she asks.

Angle sighs loudly. 'Because I belong here!'

Puddle doesn't know what to say.

Hamley doesn't know what to say either.

The three of them stand silently, looking at each other.

'Goodbye then, Angle,' says Puddle finally.

'Bye bye, Angle,' says Hamley.

The platypus and the pog disappear off into the long grass. The last thing Angle sees is Hamley's curly tail. But it's not wagging anymore.

She doesn't want to lose them. She's made a huge mistake!

'Wait! I didn't mean to—' she starts. But it's too late. They have already gone. *Oh no, what have I done?* she wonders *They are the first friends I've ever had.*

Angle stares at the long grass, wishing she could take back everything she has said. She considers running after them, but isn't sure if she could even catch them up with her little legs. She blinks heavily several times and her tail twitches.

'What are you doing here?' shouts a gruff voice from behind her.

Angle turns to find that all the alligators are glaring at her.

'Umm…I'm looking for somewhere to live, and I thought that—' Angle starts.

'Well you don't belong here! Look at your snout!' calls a female alligator from the other side of the crowd. Her voice is shrill and mean and carries across The Muddy Marsh without losing its sting.

The Mean Alligator's children, who are playing on her back, start sniggering and repeating her words: 'You don't belong here! You don't belong here!'

A couple of older alligators seem to *humph* in agreement. The rest remain quiet, but they're still staring at her.

'But I don't have anywhere else to go,' says Angle, starting to walk forward between the alligators. She tries appealing to their silent, stony faces; but as she approaches them, they slide themselves into the water, one by one, until only The Mean Alligator is left.

'Go on, a*min*al, you do not belong here. We could have eaten you. Next time, you will not be so lucky.' And she too disappears into the water. Her shrill voice echoes in Angle's ears.

Still sniggering, her children follow her into the swamp. One of them says, 'Bye bye!' cheerily.

In the water, dozens of eyes are poking above the surface, watching her.

'Please?' says Angle, feebly.

As one, the eyes disappear underwater, and she is left completely alone by the side of the swamp.

The water is smooth and still, with no sign that there are alligators lurking beneath the surface.

Angle can't help but cry. She's lost her only friends, and she still has no family. If neither the crocodiles nor the alligators will welcome her, then what hope does she have of finding anywhere to call home?

As if copying her tears, large raindrops start falling from the sky. The smooth surface of the swamp becomes dimpled and disturbed. The hard ground beneath her feet instantly softens and turns into thick, gloopy mud.

Angle now realises why it is called The Muddy Marsh. But it's not fun like she always imagined. She's cold, wet, muddy and exhausted. Mostly muddy. Very muddy.

And she's never felt so alone.

With the daylight beginning to fade, Angle needs to find shelter for the night. She plods along the side of the swamp. With each step her feet get stuck in the mud and she has to heave them out. It's very hard work. *There was never mud like this on The Cliff,* she reflects.

At last, Angle sees an old, crooked tree. At the base of it, between two large roots, is a small hollow. It is not much, but it should protect her from the worst of the wind and rain. She crawls into it and curls up into a ball, covering her snout with her tail. Despite the noise of the rain thudding the ground and slapping the mud, Angle falls almost instantly asleep and she dreams of being back in Nowhere.

Chapter 10

Baboons!

When Angle wakes up, the sun is shining, the air is warm, and there's a face a few inches from hers! The shock makes her jump and she bangs her head on the tree root. *What a perfectly horrid way to wake up!*

'Good morning,' says the face. The voice is slow and raspy. The face is long and narrow, with fierce eyes.

Angle knows what animal it belongs to. 'You're a baboon,' she states, matter-of-factly.

The face grins, showing huge sharp teeth. 'Clever girl,' it says, in that raspy voice. 'Clever, clever girl. Tell me, what's such a clever little alligator doing all on their own?'

Angle has never been frightened of anyone *else*'s teeth before. It's normally *her* teeth that *others* are afraid of. 'I'm...I'm not an...alligator,' she stutters.

The baboon apologises, but his expression doesn't seem to change. 'Pardon me, little one. Then what is such a clever little crocodile doing all on their own by The

Muddy Marsh?'

Angle's tail starts to twitch.

She remembers the Old Codgers warning her about how dangerous baboons can be. *Intelligent* and *ruthless* were the words they used. At the time, Angle thought she'd never meet any baboons, so it didn't really matter to her. But now she wishes she had listened more carefully. Before that, she had thought that baboons were silly and funny because the name *baboon* is...well, quite silly and funny.

'I am not a crocodile,' she says, trying to keep a brave face.

The baboon smirks and says, 'Not an alligator *or* a crocodile? Well, one of us has clearly woken up crazy this morning. I do hope it isn't me.'

Angle feels a rush of anger. She has left her home; she has been rejected by crocodiles, threatened by alligators and woken by a baboon; and, most importantly, she has lost her friends. 'I'm a crocogator!' she shouts. 'I am *not* a crocodile. I am *not* an alligator. I am a *crocogator*!'

For a few moments, the baboon is taken aback by her boldness. But then his horrible

grin reappears. 'Well now...an a*min*al...
how interesting. I've certainly never tried
crocogator before...'

Angle knows she needs to free herself
from the tree hollow, or she'll be trapped!
She leaps forward and snaps her jaws three
times. *Snap, snap, snap!* The baboon springs
backward, out of the way of her teeth, and
Angle tries to escape.

She can't run away though. Playing with
Puddle and Hamley made her realise how
slow she is. Her silly little slow legs! Her
only option is to try and defend herself with
her jaws. She faces the baboon and tries to
look as tough as possible, snapping her jaws
three more times. *Snap, snap, snap!*

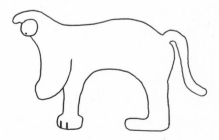

Now that she's out of the tree hollow, she can see just how large the baboon is. Why did she ever think the name *baboon* was funny?

He towers over her, with a massive head and a wide mouth, and teeth that are longer than hers. His bony, grasping hands are clenched into fists, and the short, grey hair that covers his body barely hides the strength in his arms. His face is as black as the night sky, and his yellow eyes blaze like the sun.

'You're a feisty one,' he says in his raspy voice. 'I shall enjoy eating you.'

'You leave her alone!'

A voice! A high-pitched voice.

It's Puddle, running as fast as she can towards them. She stops too abruptly and tumbles forward, landing in a heap next to Angle.

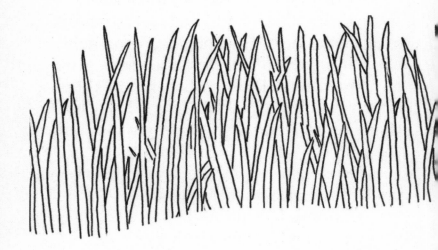

Angle is so happy to see her friend, but before she can say anything, the baboon speaks again.

'My my...what's this?' he says. '*Two* a*min*als to feast on? It's my lucky day.'

Puddle rights herself and shakes her head. Then, much to Angle's surprise, she yells at the baboon: 'I AM NOT AN A*MIN*AL!' She turns to Angle and asks, 'Why does everyone keep saying that?'

'Because you look like you're half—'

'Enough!' bellows the baboon. 'Who cares if you're an a*min*al or an animal or anything else for that matter? All you are is food.'

Angle and Puddle look at each other.

'He's right,' says Angle, quietly.

'I am not food!' replies Puddle, wobbling her head from side to side.

'No, no, not about that. About us. We are what we are. I'm an a*min*al and you're... wait, are you *sure* you're not an a*min*al?'

Puddle sighs. 'Yes, I'm sure.'

'It's just, you look like you're half—'

'I know! I'm aware of what I look like, but I'm a platypus. An animal!'

'Right, just checking,' says Angle, though she still has her doubts. 'But you see, it doesn't matter what we are, and it doesn't matter what others think about us. Wherever we come from, or whatever we look like, we are all—'

'Enough talking!' barks the baboon. 'It's dinner time and I'm hungry. And like I said, all you are is food!'

What the baboon doesn't realise though, is that he's just given Angle the most meaningful advice she's ever received. Of course, he didn't mean to do that, but sometimes advice comes from the strangest places.

Angle doesn't have time to think about it right now though, because the baboon is coming for them.

She glances behind her. She and Puddle are both good swimmers; maybe they could escape into the swamp. But she's alarmed to see several eyes watching them from the brown water.

The rasping voice speaks once again. 'Who should I eat first?' it wonders aloud. 'Who's more sweet, and who's more savoury? I think I'll go for...you!'

The baboon lunges towards Angle with his bony claws, but at that moment a

speeding blurred shape barrels into him
and he crashes into the crooked tree with a
thump!

'Hamley!' shout Angle and Puddle at the
same time.

The pog bounds over to them, slightly
unsteadily, and licks their faces. Angle
notices that his curly tail is wagging once
again.

'I didn't know where you'd gone,' says
Puddle. 'I thought you were right behind
me.'

Despite being half dog and half pig,

Hamley looks sheepish. 'I'm sorry. I saw this mushroom, and I wanted to eat it, but I couldn't reach it. So, I got this stick and—'

'Hamley, look out!' yells Angle.

The baboon has got to his feet and is dusting himself off. 'Oh how sweet, a little reunion, is it? More food for me!' he snarls, his grin wider than ever.

Hamley backs away, until he is sandwiched between Angle and Puddle. They stand in a line and face the baboon together.

'We're not scared of you!' says Angle. She feels bigger and stronger and...yes, *braver* with her friends by her side.

'Yeah, we're not scared of a silly, smirking baboon!' adds Puddle.

Hamley doesn't say anything, but growls in agreement. He would have sounded intimidating but for the accidental *oink* at the end.

The baboon looks at each of them. 'Fine, fine,' he says, backing away. 'I know when I'm outnumbered.' His grin droops into a frown.

As he turns away, Angle looks at Hamley and Puddle and smiles at each of them. She opens her mouth to speak, but before she can, the baboon suddenly starts laughing. It's an evil cackle that makes Angle's scales rattle.

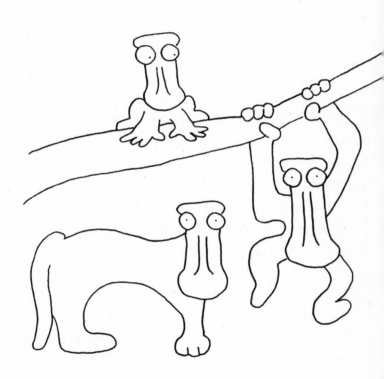

'I suppose,' shouts the baboon, spinning round, 'I'll just have to share you with my family!'

From behind him, a large group of baboons appear silently from the grass and line up either side of him. Some even climb into the branches of the crooked tree.

There must be twenty of them, thinks Angle.

'Tasty little a*min*als, meet my family! Family, meet your breakfast!' The baboon's voice seems to scrape his teeth on the way out. He makes a sweeping gesture with his arms and all the baboons start shrieking in an ear-splitting wall of noise.

Angle retreats several paces. She feels the cool water of the swamp on her tail, and looks behind her. Even more eyes are watching them from the surface of the water now.

The alligators are waiting.

Angle looks desperately from Hamley to Puddle and back again. In front of them is a screaming troop of hungry baboons. Behind them is a swamp filled with silent, hungry alligators.

They are trapped.

Chapter 11

Muddy Marsh mayhem

The baboons advance. They might attack at any second. Angle, Hamley and Puddle retreat, forced closer and closer to the swamp—closer and closer to the alligators—until their feet are in the water.

A baboon breaks rank and lunges at Puddle. She ducks just in time. The baboon flies over her head and lands in the water. With a big splash it disappears. So too do the alligators' eyes, but they soon return.

At least the other hungry baboons shouldn't attack us while we're in the water, thinks Angle. *They don't want to get eaten by the alligators either.*

Angle notices that Puddle has turned round and is quivering at the sight of the alligators in the swamp. Her duck-mouth is clattering open and shut, and her beaver-tail is twitching up and down.

Hamley is still staring straight at the baboon leader. Both of them are growling, their teeth bared. But Angle can see that Hamley's legs are shaking. His tail is curled tightly behind him, not moving at all.

They are here because of me! The thought is almost too much to bear for Angle, but what can she do to help?

'Stay in the shallows,' she says. 'Don't go deeper.' It's all she can think of.

'And then what?' asks Puddle, in her unfunny whispering voice.

Angle doesn't know. There doesn't seem

to be any way out. She feels completely helpless, but she's more scared for her friends than for herself. 'I'm sorry,' she says. 'I'm so so sorry.'

Hamley and Puddle look at her.

Angle continues, 'I'm so sorry for abandoning you. You're my only friends and I left you. You came back for me, even after I was horrid.'

'That's what friends do,' says Puddle.

'And friends have to stick together,' adds Hamley.

Angle's eyes well up and she blurts, 'And now I've got you into this mess.'

Hamley reaches out and touches her foot with his trotter. He does the same with Puddle on his other side. 'At least we're together,' he says.

At that moment, there are shouts and splashes from behind. They turn and see two creatures distracting the alligators.

'The Old Codgers!' gasps Angle. She watches Wimmy and Marlowe as they jump and swim and dive and bounce from one alligator to the next, causing an uproar in the swamp. The alligators chase after them, snapping their jaws.

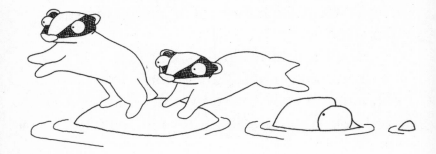

Angle has never seen the Old Codgers move so fast before! They are normally so slow and steady. She can't believe that they are here! Two little mammals using huge toothy reptiles as trampolines!

As Angle smiles, watching the two Old Codgers, something grabs her tail. It's the leader of the baboons trying to haul her out of the shallows. Her foot slips from next to Hamley's as she is pulled backwards.

'I *will* have my meal!' declares the baboon, in that scratchy voice.

'No you will not!' shouts Puddle, and she launches herself at him. Her duck-mouth clamps onto his arm and makes him drop

Angle's tail.

Hamley is next to spring into action. He hurls himself at the baboon and grabs one of his legs between his teeth.

'Pull him into the deeper water,' yells Angle. She then snaps her jaws closed onto the baboon's other leg. His fur tickles the roof of her mouth, but she doesn't let go.

The baboon howls and tries to free himself from their grip, but the three friends thrust their tails and legs through the water and force him away from the shore.

We're stronger together, Angle suddenly realises.

'You stupid crocodile!' the baboon snarls, spit flying from his mouth. 'Even the three of you are no match for me.' He brings his free arm down heavily on Angle's back, knocking the breath out of her. He raises his arm again, and Angle braces herself...

But the blow never comes. Instead, the baboon shrieks as a large alligator appears beside them and grabs his free arm between its powerful jaws.

Angle immediately lets go and tells the others to do the same. They just have time to see the baboon being dragged away, before it disappears into the murky depths.

The troop of baboons wail and retreat into the grass. Without their leader, they are lost.

Before Angle can even think about what has just happened, Marlowe, the male odger, appears beside them and shouts, 'Go! Get out of the swamp!'

Angle, Puddle and Hamley start swimming towards the land, but before they reach it, an alligator surfaces between them and the shore.

Angle immediately recognises it as The Mean Alligator from the day before.

'I'm glad you've come back!' says the alligator in her shrill voice. 'I'm hungry.' Her broad snout snaps open and shut.

A shadow starts to fall over her head, growing bigger and bigger, darker and darker.

Feathers and wings and webbed feet land on The Mean Alligator's head with a heavy slap. It's Tupi the toulican! 'Go now! I'll deal with this,' he shouts. He then performs what can only be described as a slap dance on the alligator's head.

Angle swims faster than she's ever swum before. She thrashes her tail and leaps from the water like a dolphin, landing on the shore. Puddle and Hamley are right behind her and they all clamber onto the land, out of breath and exhausted. Seconds later, the Old Codgers and Tupi land beside them in a shower of water.

'Come on,' says Wimmy, ushering them

further away from the swamp. 'Those alligators may only have little legs, but they can still use them.' She then adds, 'No offence, Angle dear.'

'You saved us!' cries Angle.

'Well it was just lucky you left a message with Spriglet,' says Marlowe.

'But…but I didn't,' states Angle.

'Well Spriglet heard you say you were leaving,' he replies. 'And we knew there were only two places we needed to look. We were terribly afraid that the crocodiles had eaten you, so we were pleased to see you here. Even if you were in a spot of bother.' He smiles warmly at her. 'It was the puffickens that actually spotted you first.'

Angle looks upwards and sees the three puffickens circling above them. She's never seen them properly fly before, but here they are! And the Old Codgers! And Tupi! And Puddle and Hamley, who came back for her.

Angle is lost for words.

'You've had quite an adventure,' says Marlowe.

'Yes, well that's all very well,' fusses Wimmy, 'but you shouldn't have run off like that. Oh I'm just so pleased you're safe.' She strolls to Angle's side and hugs her tightly.

Angle sighs and relaxes against Wimmy's comfortable thick fur.

But a raspy, uncomfortable voice shouts, 'Why couldn't you have just been good little meals!'

The huge snarling shape of the baboon emerges from the swamp and staggers towards them. He stands up tall and shakes the water from his fur. His eyes are burning and his sharp teeth are glinting in the light. One of his arms hangs limply by his side.

'I just wanted to eat you,' he spits. 'Is that really so much to ask?'

Angle ambles forwards. With her friends around her, she feels a courage she's never felt before. 'We are not afraid of you.'

The baboon stares at her. And to her surprise, he grins. That ugly, evil grin again. 'You should be,' he warns. 'Attack!'

The grass behind them explodes as the other baboons burst back onto the scene and overwhelm the aminals. They grab the squirming odgers with their strong arms.

One of them pins Tupi down before he can fly away. Three of them grapple Hamley to the ground. Puddle is picked up by her beaver-tail. Her wriggling body can't free itself from the clutches of the baboon's bony hand.

The leader laughs. 'You see, little crocodile, you are nothing but food after all.' He reaches out to grab her; but, as he does, the ground begins to tremble. 'What's this?' he says, scowling.

Hamley oinks loudly. 'You've met...' He is struggling under his captors. 'You've met Angle and Puddle, but it's time for you to meet the *rest* of my family!'

Right on cue, a pig, a dog and a huge group of pogs tumble out of the grass, their trotters hammering the ground as they charge at the baboons, who screech and scatter.

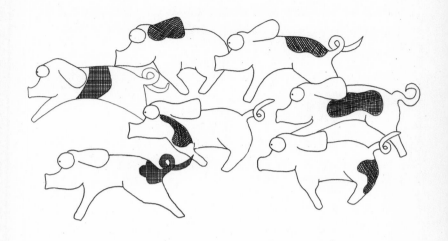

The Old Codgers and Tupi are released. Hamley wrestles himself free. Puddle is dropped. The baboons' cries grow fainter as they flee. Only their leader remains.

Angle faces him. Puddle and Hamley join her, one either side.

'I was right all along,' says Angle. 'Baboons are silly animals.'

The baboon snarls at her as he starts to slowly walk away. 'I will see you again, little crocodile. And next time, you won't have these unnatural *misfits* to protect you.'

'I'm a crocogator!' Angle shouts after him. 'And they are not misfits…they are my family!'

Chapter 12

Back in Nowhere

After journeying back together, Angle, Puddle and Hamley arrive in Nowhere, along with their rescue party. As soon as Hamley's family see the open land at the top of The Cliff, and the beautiful views, they can't imagine living anywhere else.

'Can we stay?' asks Hamley, jumping up and down. 'Please can we stay?'

So they decide to settle on The Cliff, and make it their home. And the village of Nowhere spreads onto the land, if only by a little.

WELCOME TO NOWHERE
POPULATION: ~~THE~~ 154 ANIMALS   189 SPECIES
              4 ANIMALS   4 SPECIES

IF YOU DON'T HAVE WINGS
BEWARE THE DROP

Angle is happy to get back to her ledge. The Always Pond is comforting and safe, and she now has a friend to share it with. Puddle feels instantly at home in Nowhere; and, for the first time in a long time, she feels like she fits in.

Hamley has just left them to return to his family above The Cliff, with the promise that he will return tomorrow. The Old Codgers have wished them a goodnight and made their way back to The Sometimes Pond. Angle knows that she will see them much more from now on.

Beside The Always Pond, a furry boulder, which has finally caught up with Angle, is curled in a ball, snoring gently.

The crocogator and the platypus float on the surface of the clear water, gazing out at The Forever Pond, an aminal and an animal, side by side.

Angle has friends and she has a family, and, now that they are all together, she doesn't want to be Elsewhere. Nowhere finally feels like home.

The light is just beginning to dim. The ocean is a deep green. Angle's eyes feel heavy with tiredness. As she slowly starts to drift off to sleep, she hears a gulping noise.

She opens her eyes to see the snortoise
standing at the edge of The Always Pond.

They stare at each other for a few
moments, and then he gulps several times
more. Eventually he gets his words out.

'Good to have you back, Angle.'

On the
Origin
of
Aminals

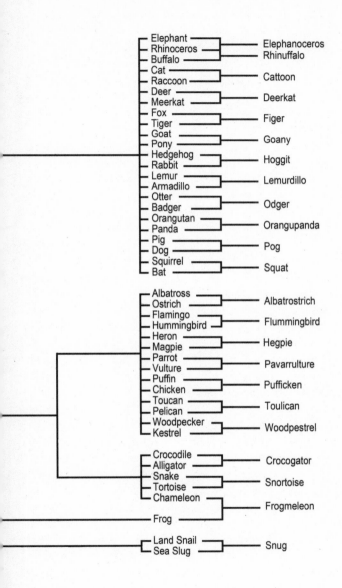